ASTERIX
IN CORSICA

TEXT BY GOSCINNY

DRAWINGS BY UDERZO

TRANSLATED BY ANTHEA BELL AND DEREK HOCKRIDGE

HODDER DARGAUD
LONDON SYDNEY AUCKLAND

ASTERIX IN OTHER COUNTRIES

Australia	Hodder Dargaud, Rydalmere Business Park, 10/16 South Street, Rydalmere, N.S.W. 2116, Australia
Austria	Delta Verlag GmbH, Postfach 10 12 45, 70011 Stuttgart, Germany
Belarus	Egmont Belarus, Mogilevskaya 43, 220007 Minsk, Belarus
Belgium	Dargaud Benelux, 17 Avenue Paul Henri Spaak, 1070 Brussels, Belgium
Brazil	Record Distribuidora, Rua Argentina 171, 20921 Rio de Janeiro, Brazil
Bulgaria	Egmont Bulgaria Ltd., U1. Sweta Gora 7, IV et.,1421 Sofia, Bulgaria
Canada	(*French*) Presse-Import Leo Brunelle Inc., 5757 rue Cypihot, St. Laurent, QC, H4S 1X4, Canada
	(*English*) General Publishing Co. Ltd., 30 Lesmill Road, Don Mills, Ontario M38 2T6, Canada
Corsica	Dargaud Editeur, 6 rue Gager Gabillot, 75015 Paris, France
Croatia	Izvori Publishing House, Trnjanska 47, 4100 Zagreb, Croatia
Czech Republic	Egmont CR, Hellichova 45, 118 00 Prague 1, Czech Republic
Denmark	Serieforlaget A/S (Egmont Group), Vognmagergade 11, 1148 Copenhagen K, Denmark
Estonia	Egmont Estonia Ltd., Hobujaamal, EE 0001 Tallinn, Estonia
Finland	Sanoma Corporation/Helsinki Media, POB 107, 00381 Helsinki, Finland
France	Dargaud Editeur, 6 rue Gager Gabillot, 75015 Paris, France
	(*titles up to and including Asterix in Belgium*)
	Les Editions Albert Rene, 26 Avenue Victor Hugo, 75116 Paris, France
	(*titles from Asterix and the Great Divide onwards*)
Germany	Delta Verlag GmbH, Postfach 10 12 45, 70011 Stuttgart, Germany
Greece	(*Ancient and Modern Greek*) Mamouth Comix Ltd., 44 Ippokratous St., 106080 Athens, Greece
Holland	Dargaud Benelux, 17 Avenue Paul Henri Spaak, 1070 Brussels, Belgium
	(*Distribution*) Betapress, Burg. Krollaan 14, 5126 PT Jilze, Holland
Hong Kong	(*English*) Hodder Dargaud, c/o Publishers Associates Ltd., 11th Floor, Taikoo Trading Estate, 28 Tong Cheong Street, Quarry Bay, Hong Kong
	(*Mandarin and Cantonese*) Gast, Fairyland Garden 6A, Broadcast Drive 8, Kowloon Tong, Hong Kong
Hungary	Egmont Hungary Kft., Karolina ut. 65, 1113 Budapest, Hungary
India	(*Bengali*) Ananda Publishers, 45 Beniatola Lane, Calcutta 700 009, India
Indonesia	PT. Pustaka Sinar Harapan, Jl. Dewi Sartika 136D, Cawang, Jakarta 13630, Indonesia
Israel	Dahlia Pelled Publishers Ltd., Pinsker 64, Tel Aviv 61116, Israel
Italy	Mondadori, Via A. Mondadori 15, 37131 Verona, Italy
Republic of Korea	Cosmos Editions, 19–16 Shin An-dong, Jin-ju, Gyung Nam-do, Republic of Korea
Latin America	Grijalbo-Dargaud, Aragon 385, 08013 Barcelona, Spain
Latvia	Egmont Latvia Ltd., Balasta Dambis 3, Room 1812, 226081 Riga, Latvia
Lithuania	Egmont Lithuania, Juozapaviciaus 9 A, Room 910/911, 2600 Vilnius, Lithuania
Luxembourg	Imprimerie St. Paul, rue Christophe Plantin 2, Luxembourg
New Zealand	Hodder Dargaud, P.O. Box 3858, Auckland 1, New Zealand
Norway	A/S Hjemmet – Serieforlaget, PB 6853 St. Olavs Pl. 0130 Oslo, Norway
Poland	Egmont Polska Ltd., Plac Marszalka J. Pilsudskiego 9, 00–078 Warsaw, Poland
Portugal	Meriberica-Liber, Av. Alvares Cabral 84, R/C-D 1200 Lisbon, Portugal
Roman Empire	(*Latin*) Delta Verlag GmbH, Postfach 10 12 45, 70011 Stuttgart, Germany
Romania	Egmont Romania S.R.L., Calea Grivitei 160, Ap. 47; Cod 78214, Sector 1, Bucharest, Romania
Russia	Egmont Russia, 9, 1st Smolenski per. 121099 Moscow, Russia
Slovak Republic	Egmont Neografia Nevädzova 8, Box 20, 82799 Bratislava 27, Slovak Republic
Slovenia	Didakta, Radovljica Kranjska Cesta 13, 64240 Radovljica, Slovenia
South Africa	(*English*) Hodder Dargaud, c/o Struik Book Distributors (Pty) Ltd., Graph Avenue, Montague Gardens 7441, South Africa
	(*Afrikaans*) Human & Rousseau (Pty) Ltd., State House, 3–9 Rose Street, Cape Town 8000, South Africa
Spain	(*Castillian, Catalan, Basque*) Grijalbo-Dargaud, Aragon 385, 08013 Barcelona, Spain
Sweden	Serieförlaget Svenska AB (Egmont Group), 212 05 Malmö, Sweden
Switzerland	Dargaud (Suisse) S.A., En Budron B-13, 1052 Le Mont sur Lausanne, Switzerland
Turkey	Remzi Kitabevi, Selvili Mescit S. 3, Cagaloglu-Istanbul, Turkey
USA	(*English and French language distributor*) Presse-Import Leo Brunelle Inc., 5757 rue Cypihot, St. Laurent, QC, H4S 1X4, Canada

Asterix in Corsica

ISBN 0 340 24074 1 (cased)
ISBN 0 340 27754 8 (limp)

Copyright © Dargaud Editeur 1973, Goscinny-Uderzo
English language text copyright © Hodder and Stoughton Ltd 1980
(now Hodder Children's Books)

First published in Great Britain 1980 (cased)
This impression 95 96 97 98

First published in Great Britain 1982 (limp)
This impression 95 96 97 98

Published by Hodder Dargaud Ltd,
338 Euston Road, London NW1 3BH

Printed in Belgium by Proost International Book Production

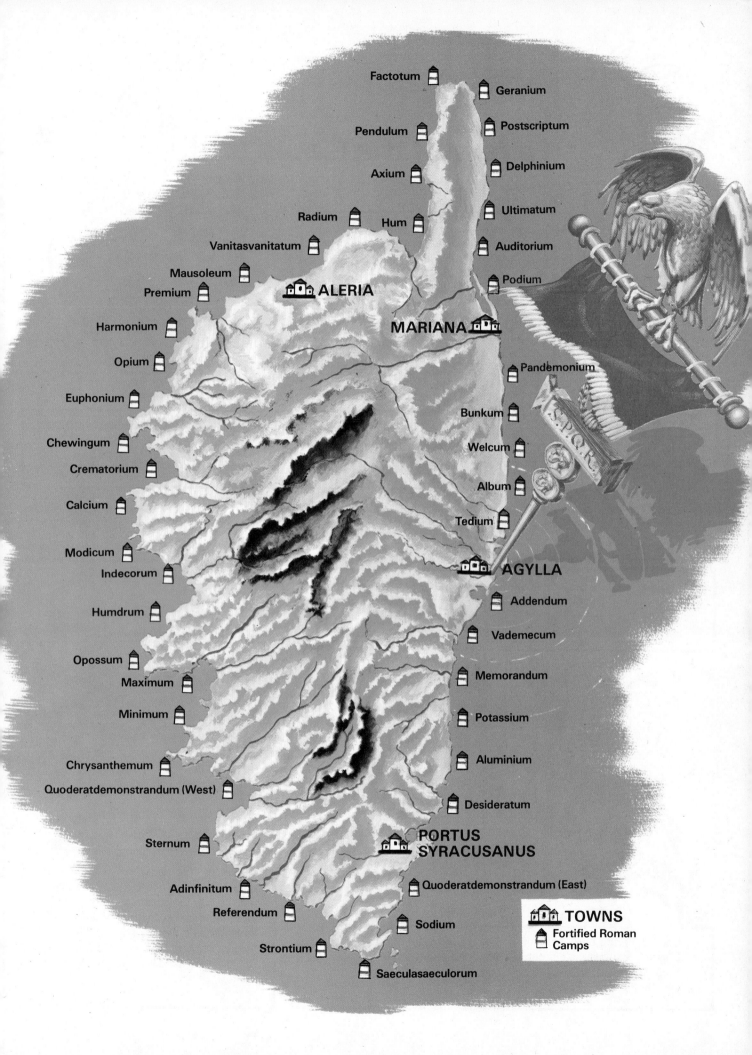

Factotum

Geranium

Pendulum

Postscriptum

Axium

Delphinium

Radium

Hum

Ultimatum

Vanitasvanitatum

Auditorium

Mausoleum

Podium

Premium

ALERIA

Harmonium

MARIANA

Opium

Pandemonium

Euphonium

Bunkum

Chewingum

Welcum

Crematorium

Album

Calcium

Tedium

Modicum

AGYLLA

Indecorum

Addendum

Humdrum

Vademecum

Opossum

Memorandum

Maximum

Potassium

Minimum

Aluminium

Chrysanthemum

Quoderatdemonstrandum (West)

Desideratum

Sternum

PORTUS SYRACUSANUS

Adinfinitum

Quoderatdemonstrandum (East)

Referendum

Sodium

Strontium

Saeculasaeculorum

TOWNS

Fortified Roman Camps

a few of the Gauls

Asterix, the hero of these adventures. A shrewd, cunning little warrior; all perilous missions are immediately entrusted to him. Asterix gets his superhuman strength from the magic potion brewed by the druid Getafix...

Obelix, Asterix's inseparable friend. A menhir delivery-man by trade; addicted to wild boar. Obelix is always ready to drop everything and go off on a new adventure with Asterix — so long as there's wild boar to eat, and plenty of fighting.

Getafix, the venerable village druid. Gathers mistletoe and brews magic potions. His speciality is the potion which gives the drinker superhuman strength. But Getafix also has other recipes up his sleeve...

Cacofonix, the bard. Opinion is divided as to his musical gifts. Cacofonix thinks he's a genius. Everyone else thinks he's unspeakable. But so long as he doesn't speak, let alone sing, everybody likes him...

Finally, Vitalstatistix, the chief of the tribe. Majestic, brave and hot-tempered, the old warrior is respected by his men and feared by his enemies. Vitalstatistix himself has only one fear; he is afraid the sky may fall on his head tomorrow. But as he always says, 'Tomorrow never comes.'

IN THE FORTIFIED ROMAN CAMP OF TOTORUM...

RIGHT! EVERYONE READY?

AND ABOUT TIME TOO! FORWARD MARCH... AND IN SILENCE, PLEASE.

?

I'M ON A MISSION, CENTURION. WE'VE COME A LONG WAY. I WANT SHELTER FOR THE NIGHT BEFORE WE CONTINUE OUR JOURNEY.

THE FACT IS... WE WERE JUST GOING OUT.

BONG!

HOW MANY OF YOU? WHERE?

ER... ALL OF US. GOING ON MANOEUVRES IN THE HINTERLAND.

YOU MEAN YOU'RE LEAVING THE CAMP UNGUARDED?

ER... SORT OF...

ARE WE OFF, CENTURION?

WHAT ARE WE WAITING FOR, BY JUPITER?

TIME'S GETTING ON!

WELL, I'M AWFULLY SORRY AND ALL THAT... DROP US A SLAB IN ADVANCE ANOTHER TIME. AVE. WE'RE OFF.

NO ONE'S OFF ANY-WHERE!

I AM ON A SPECIAL MISSION FROM PRAETOR PERFIDIUS, GOVERNOR OF CORSICA, AND I DEMAND AN EXPLANATION OF THIS SUSPICIOUS HASTE!

LISTEN, CENTURION HIPPOPOTAMUS, IF YOU DON'T MIND WE'LL GO ON AHEAD AND YOU JOIN US LATER, ALL RIGHT?

NO, IT IS NOT ALL RIGHT!

HERE, COME INTO MY TENT... DON'T START WITHOUT ME, YOU LOT. THIS WON'T TAKE LONG.

?

TODAY IS THE ANNIVERSARY OF THE BATTLE OF GERGOVIA. THE PEOPLE OF THE NEARBY GAULISH VILLAGE HAVE A WAY OF CELEBRATING THE OCCASION BY ATTACKING THE NEIGHBOURING ROMAN GARRISONS.

AND YOU DON'T ATTEMPT TO STOP THIS LOCAL CUSTOM?

WE CERTAINLY DO! WE STOP IT BY LEAVING CAMP AND GOING ON MANOEUVRES!

ARE YOU READY, CENTURION HIPPOPOTAMUS? THE BOYS ARE GETTING A BIT IMPATIENT, AND...

ARE THESE GAULS REALLY SO FEROCIOUS?

WELL, TOO BAD. I'M ESCORTING A CORSICAN EXILE, AND HE'S SPENDING THE NIGHT IN THIS CAMP. YOU AND YOUR GARRISON ARE RESPONSIBLE TO CAESAR FOR HIS SAFE KEEPING. I'LL BE BACK TO PICK HIM UP TOMORROW.

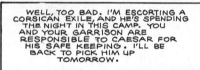

TOMORROW? WHERE ARE YOU GOING TODAY?

TO JOIN IN THE MANOEUVRES, OF COURSE!

BUT... BUT YOU CAN'T DO THIS TO US! THE GAULS WILL SLAUGHTER US! WHAT'S MORE, IF THEY SEE WE'VE GOT A PRISONER HERE, THEY'LL...

BRING THE EXILE ALONG!

AVE, CENTURION, AND DON'T FORGET, CAESAR WILL HOLD YOU RESPONSIBLE!

THE FIRST GUESTS ARE ARRIVING AT THE LITTLE GAULISH VILLAGE...

PETITSUIX!

I'VE BROUGHT YOU A HELVETIAN CHEESE.

HUEVOS Y BACON!

¡OLE, HOMBRES, OLÉ!

¡DOGMATIX!

INSTANTMIX! YOU'VE COME ALL THE WAY FROM ROME!

I JUST HAD TO HEAR THE SOUND OF YOUR VOICE AGAIN!

ANTICLIMAX! MYKINGDOMFORANOS! O'VEROPTIMISTIX! McANIX! DIPSOMANIAX!

I SAY, OLD BOY, THIS IS SIMPLY MARVELLOUS, WHAT? GOOD TO SEE YOU, COUSIN ASTERIX!

JELLIBABIX FROM LUGDUNUM! DRINKLIKAFIX FROM MASSILIA! SENIORSERVIX FROM GESOCRIBATUM!

WINESANSPIRIX THE ARVERNIAN!

REMEMBER HOW WE DIDDLED CAESAR OUT OF THE CHIEFTAIN'S SHIELD?

WHAT A PRETTY DRESS!

YES, IT'S MADE OF OUR OWN *LUGDUNUM SILK.

*LYONS

I'M ENJOYING BEING LIONISED LIKE THIS TOO.

¡HOMBRE! ¡I USE OLIVE OIL FOR ALL MY COOKING!

YOU DON'T SAY! FANCY THAT! I USE BOILING WATER. IT GIVES EVERYTHING A LOVELY FLAVOUR, DON'T YOU KNOW?

REMEMBER HOW WE BOWLED THOSE ROMANS OVER IN MASSILIA?

HAHAHAHA!

REMEMBER WHEN YOU WERE EATING HOLES IN CHEESE IN THAT GENEVA BANK VAULT?

AN ARMED VIGIL IS IN PROGRESS AT TOTORUM ...

...AND THERE'LL BE THE GREAT BIG BRUTE, AND THE DREADFUL LITTLE MIDGET, ALL STUFFED WITH MAGIC POTION, AND THEY WON'T LIKE IT WHEN THEY SEE WE'VE GOT A PRISONER EITHER ...

CHATTER CHATTER CHATTER

CHATTER CHATTER CHATTER

OH NO, BY JUPITER! THIS IS TOO MUCH!

CHATTER CHATTER

LISTEN, I'M GOING TO UNLOCK YOUR CHAINS ...

IF THEY RECAPTURE YOU, YOU MUST PROMISE TO SAY YOU ESCAPED ON YOUR OWN AND NO ONE HELPED YOU ... DON'T ASK WHY I'M DOING THIS FOR YOU ...

!CLICK!

8A

YOU CAN GO! YOU'RE FREE!

I SAID: YOU CAN GO! YOU'RE FREE!

LISTEN, WILL YOU? YOU'RE FREE! YOU CAN GO!

AFTER MY SIESTA.

WHAT DO YOU MEAN, AFTER YOUR SIESTA?

IT'S GETTING LATE, ROMAN. IF I DON'T HAVE MY SIESTA NOW, I SHAN'T HAVE TIME TO HAVE IT BEFORE BEDTIME, SO LEAVE ME ALONE OR I MIGHT LOSE MY TEMPER.

LOOK, ARE YOU OR ARE YOU NOT GOING TO ESCAPE?!

THEY'RE COMING, CENTURION HIPPOPOTAMUS, AND THEY'VE GOT SOME FRIENDS WITH THEM. WE WOULDN'T LIKE YOU TO MISS THE START.

8B

14

RIGHT, THAT'S SETTLED! TOMORROW MORNING ASTERIX AND OBELIX WILL LEAVE FOR CORSICA WITH YOU. WHEN THEY COME BACK THEY CAN TELL US WHAT METHODS YOU CORSICANS USE, AND WHAT YOUR COUNTRY'S LIKE!

NEXT MORNING...

I SAY, OLD FRUIT, YOU DO A GOOD LINE IN PARTIES!

YES, MARVELLOUS PARTY LINE!

SUCH LIBERALITY! OUR TASTES ARE CONSERVATIVE, BUT YOU DIDN'T LABOUR IN VAIN!

SMACK!

AND JUST WHY SHOULDN'T I TAKE HIM?

HERE WE GO AGAIN! BECAUSE HE'S TOO SMALL, THAT'S WHY!

WE'VE BEEN LOOKING FOR YOU EVERYWHERE, BOYS. YOU'D BETTER LEAVE BEFORE THE ROMANS COME BACK. DON'T FORGET, OUR CORSICAN FRIEND IS IN GREAT DEMAND.

GRUMBLE-GRUMBLE-GRUMBLE...

GNAGNAGNA GNA GNAGNA...

AND HERE'S A GOURD OF MAGIC POTION FOR YOU TOO, BONEYWASAWARRIOR-WAYAYIX. A USEFUL LITTLE GIFT AS A MEMENTO OF YOUR VISIT TO US.

JUST A MINUTE! I'VE GOT A USEFUL LITTLE GIFT FOR YOU TOO!

?

A LITTLE DOG! I'M VERY FOND OF DOGS!

IT MEANS I CAN TRAVEL LIGHT, TOO. HE'LL HAVE TO CARRY DOGMATIX, AND DOGMATIX HAS BEEN PUTTING ON A BIT OF WEIGHT LATELY...

OH, VERY CLEVER, OBELIX!

YOU DON'T CATCH US BONY CHARACTERS NAPPING, ASTERIX-OCELLIX!

THE PORT OF MASSILIA...

I MUST FIND A BOAT TO TAKE US TO CORSICA. I HAVE FRIENDS IN MASSILIA. WHO'LL HELP ME, BUT I'D BETTER GO ON MY OWN.

WE'LL MEET HERE IN AN HOUR'S TIME. HOLD THIS DOG FOR ME, I'M RATHER TIRED.

VERMICELLIX

13

BONEYWASA-WARRIORWAYAYIX, I AM BESIDE MYSELF WITH JOY.

VERMICELLIX, THE SIGHT OF YOU FILLS ME WITH PLEASURE.

MORTADELLA, LET'S HAVE SOME WINE AND SOME SAUSAGE. NOT THE STUFF WE GIVE THE CUSTOMERS.

13

NOW, GO AND SEE TO THE CUSTOMERS.

MPH.

THIS SAUSAGE BRINGS BACK MEMORIES OF MY NATIVE LAND! SO FRESH YOU CAN ALMOST HEAR IT BRAYING.

STILL PRETTY, AS YOU CAN SEE, BUT SHE JUST CAN'T KEEP HER MOUTH SHUT. WELL, THAT'S ENOUGH ABOUT WOMEN. I THOUGHT YOU WERE IN EXILE?

CLICK!

NOT ANY MORE. YOU MUST FIND ME A BOAT TO CROSS BACK TO CORSICA.

IT WON'T BE EASY. THE ROMANS ARE WATCHING THE PORT. BUT I'VE GOT SOME SAILORS IN THERE WHO SEEM TO BE PRETTY COOL CUSTOMERS. COME ON.

ANYTHING ELSE YOU FANCY?

NOT A SAUSAGE, EH, CAP'N?

14A

I'D LIKE TO MAKE YOU AN OFFER. WILL YOU TAKE SOME MEN ON BOARD FOR CORSICA? VERY DISCREETLY. NAME YOUR PRICE.

THE PRICE IS RIGHT, BUT THEY'LL NEED GOLD FOR SHIPBOARD EXPENSES.

SOON AFTERWARDS...

WELL, THAT'S FIXED. WE EMBARK TONIGHT. COME ON, I KNOW SOMEWHERE WE CAN HAVE A SIESTA.

TCHAC!

HEY, YOU!

?

SEE?

HARRGH HARRGH HARRGH! PASSENGERS, WITH LOTS OF GOLD. ONCE AT SEA, WE'LL CLEAN THEM OUT AND MAKE THEM WALK THE PLANK. NO MORE BOARDING SHIPS FOR US, WE'RE GOING IN FOR OVERBOARDING!

O TEMPORA, O MORES!

AND MORE'S THE WORD.

14B

NEXT MORNING...

NO ONE AROUND! THEY'VE ABANDONED SHIP!

WELL, NEVER MIND. JUDGING BY THE SUN, WE'RE ON THE RIGHT COURSE FOR CORSICA.

BUT I'M HUNGRY!

SNIFF! SNIFF!

COME ON, THEN! VERMICELLIX GAVE ME A CORSICAN CHEESE. YOU'LL FIND IT'S QUITE SOMETHING!

16A

TAKE A SNIFF AT THAT, FRIENDS!

I...I THINK I'LL JUST GO AND LIE DOWN...

FLICK!

HOWL! HOWL! HOWL!

16B

AH, THAT AROMA...

SNIFF! SNIFF!

SUCH A DELICATE, SUBTLE AROMA, CALLING TO MIND THYME AND ALMOND TREES, FIG TREES, CHESTNUT TREES... AND THEN AGAIN, THE FAINTEST HINT OF PINES, A TOUCH OF TARRAGON, A SUGGESTION OF ROSEMARY AND LAVENDER... AH, MY FRIENDS, THAT AROMA...

...IS THE ESSENCE OF CORSICA!

CORSICA!

THESE CORSICANS ARE CRAZY!

OH, COME ON, LET'S FOLLOW HIM.

TAP! TAP! TAP!

SPLASH!

SPLASH!

SPLASH!

SMELL THAT WATER! THAT MARVELLOUS SCENT OF LOBSTER, SEA URCHIN AND SHRIMP!

PERSONALLY, I THINK IT SMELLS OF ROMANS... ISN'T THAT A FORTIFIED ROMAN CAMP OVER THERE?

YES, THERE ARE CAMPS ALL ROUND THE SHORES OF THE ISLANDS. IT'S WHEN THEY TRY GETTING INTO THE MAQUIS IN THE INTERIOR THE ROMANS HAVE PROBLEMS.

BUT DON'T WORRY. THE ROMANS WHO GET SENT HERE ARE USUALLY A POOR LOT, POSTED TO CORSICA BY WAY OF PUNISHMENT. IT'S ONLY THE PRAETOR WHO KEEPS A FEW CRACK TROOPS AT ALERIA.

SEE THAT? WE'D BETTER LET THE CENTURION KNOW!

YEAH... ANYWAY, DON'T LET'S HANG AROUND HERE.

HURRY UP, CAN'T YOU?

TAKE IT EASY NOW... JUST TAKE IT EASY!

YOU'RE NEW HERE, SO TAKE IT VERY, VERY EASY AND I'LL EXPLAIN THINGS.

21

22

23

ISN'T THAT LITTLE BONEYWASA-WARRIOR-WAYAYIX WHO WENT TO THE CONTINENT?

YES. I KNEW THEY WOULDN'T WANT TO KEEP HIM.

THE OTHES AREN'T LOCALS. LOOK AT THAT DOG, HE'S NO BIGGER THAN A BLACKBIRD.

HE DOESN'T GET ENOUGH SIESTA.

OH, LOOK! TAME BOARS!

NO, THOSE ARE WILD PIGS.

CHIEF BONEYWASA-WARRIORWAYAYIX! YOU'RE BACK!

PLEASED TO SEE YOU, CARFERRIX.

TO THINK WE WERE JUST ABOUT TO HOLD ELECTIONS FOR A NEW CHIEF. THE BALLOT BOXES ARE ALREADY FULL.

YOU MEAN THE BALLOT BOXES ARE FULL BEFORE THE ELECTION'S HELD?

YES, BUT WE THROW THEM INTO THE SEA WITHOUT OPENING THEM, AND THEN THE STRONGEST MAN WINS. IT'S AN OLD CORSICAN CUSTOM.

MEET ASTERIX, OBELIX AND DOGMATIX. THEY'VE COME TO SEE HOW WE CORSICANS DEAL WITH THE ROMANS.

WHY NOT COME AND HAVE SOME WILD PIG AT MY PLACE?

25

LOOK, NO BIGGER THAN A CHESTNUT, BUT HE EATS AS IF HIS SIESTA DEPENDED ON IT!

SCRUNCH! SCRUNCH!

WELL, HOW ARE THINGS GOING?

THE WAREHOUSES OF ALERIA ARE FULL OF THE LOOT PRAETOR PERFIDIUS HAS TAKEN. THERE ISN'T MUCH TIME LEFT, THE PRAETOR WILL SOON BE RECALLED TO ROME.

THEN WHY NOT ATTACK NOW?

ALERIA IS WELL DEFENDED. WE NEED TIME TO SUMMON EVERYONE FROM THE OTHER VILLAGES. THAT'S WHAT I WAS DOING WHEN I WAS CAPTURED IN OLABELLA-MARGARITIX'S VILLAGE.

CRRiiii

OLABELLA-MARGARITIX?

MY CLAN AND OLABELLAMARGARITIX'S CLAN HAVE A VENDETTA GOING, BUT I NEVER THOUGHT HE'D BETRAY ME TO THE ROMANS.

THERE'S NO PROOF HE DID...

THE OLABELLAMARGARITIX CLAN ARE CAPABLE OF ANYTHING!

WHAT'S THE VENDETTA ABOUT?

NO ONE'S TOO SURE ANY MORE...

THE OLD FOLK SAY BONEYWASAWARRIORWAYAYIX'S GREAT-UNCLE MARRIED A GIRL FROM THE VIOLONCELLIX CLAN, AND A COUSIN BY MARRIAGE OF ONE OF OLABELLAMARGARITIX'S GRANDFATHERS WAS IN LOVE WITH HER...

BUT OTHERS SAY IT WAS BECAUSE OF A DONKEY WHICH OLABELLAMARGARITIX'S GREAT-GRANDFATHER REFUSED TO PAY FOR WHEN BONEY A CLOSE FRIEND OF THE CLAIMASAWARRIORWAYAYIX CLAN, DONKEY THAT HE WAS LAME (THE WARR NOT THE BONEYWASA-RWAYAYIXES' FRIEND'S BROCHER-IN-LAW)...

...ANYWAY, IT'S VERY SERIOUS.

TAP! TAP! TAP!

?

22

ALERIA...

A LEGIONARY TO SEE YOU, O PRAETOR PERFIDIUS. HE SAYS HE HAS IMPORTANT INFORMATION.

SHOW HIM IN.

AVE, PRAETOR! THIS MAN WANTS TO SPIN YOU A YARN.

NO, I DON'T! I'M AN HONEST SAILOR WORKING THE MASSILIA-CORSICA CROSSING...

CLAC!

I TOOK THREE PASSENGERS ON BOARD, AND BEFORE THEY DISAPPEARED THEY BLEW UP MY SHIP WITH AN INFERNAL DEVICE IN THE FORM OF A CHEESE...

A CORSICAN CHEESE?

234

ANYWAY, ONE OF THE PASSENGERS WAS CORSICAN... THEY CALLED HIM BONEYWASAWARRIOR POMTIDDLYPOM.

WAYAYIX?!

YES, THAT'S RIGHT. NOT POMTIDDLYPOM, WAYAYIX. THERE WERE TWO GAULS WITH HIM, TWO REAL THREATS TO SHIPPING WHO...

WHERE DID THEY GO?

I SAW THEM MAKE OFF INLAND, TOWARDS THE MOUNTAINS. I REQUEST THE HONOUR OF PARTICIPATING IN THE SEARCH IF THESE MEN ARE OUTLAWS.

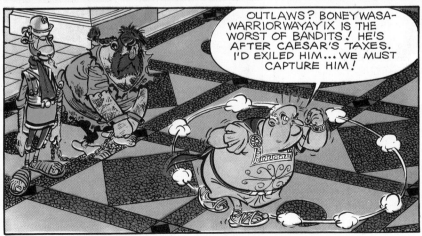

OUTLAWS? BONEYWASA-WARRIORWAYAYIX IS THE WORST OF BANDITS! HE'S AFTER CAESAR'S TAXES. I'D EXILED HIM...WE MUST CAPTURE HIM!

O PRAETOR, I WILL RECAPTURE BONEYWAS WARRIORHEYNONNYN

WAYAY

BONG!

YOU'RE COURTING-DISASTUS...

YES, I VOLUNTEERED TO COME TO CORSICA. I HEARD CHANCES OF PROMOTION WERE GOOD.

RIGHT! I APPOINT YOU LEADER OF THE PATROL WHICH IS GOING AFTER THE BANDIT. HIS VILLAGE IS THE FIRST ON THE LEFT AS YOU GO UP THE VALLEY.

I'LL NEED SOME MEN.

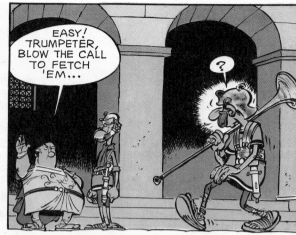

EASY! TRUMPETER, BLOW THE CALL TO FETCH 'EM...

?

COME TO THE COOKHOUSE DOOR, BOYS!!!

24

EXCELLENT! THE FIRST TEN MEN HAVE VOLUNTEERED TO GO AND RECAPTURE BONEYWASA-WARRIORWAYAYIX!

I TOLD YOU, YOU FOOL, DIDN'T I? WE'D ONLY JUST HAD A MEAL!

YOU WERE RIGHT ...I HADN'T EVEN FINISHED EATING.

I'LL BRING BACK THE BANDIT, PRAETOR. AVE!

CLAC!

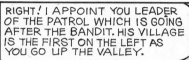
27

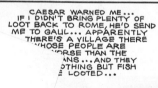
33

CAESAR WARNED ME... IF I DIDN'T BRING PLENTY OF LOOT BACK TO ROME, HE'D SEND ME TO GAUL... APPARENTLY THERE'S A VILLAGE THERE WHOSE PEOPLE ARE WORSE THAN THE CORSICANS... AND THEY HAVE NOTHING BUT FISH TO BE LOOTED...

AND I'VE HEARD IT ISN'T ALWAYS FRESH EITHER!

24

30

34

THE CORSICANS ARE GOING TO ATTACK ALERIA AND RAID THE WAREHOUSES...

YEAH?

SO, VERY DISCREETLY, YOU ARE GOING TO MOVE THE CONTENTS OF THE WAREHOUSES AND GET THEM ON BOARD THE BIG GALLEY OUT IN THE HARBOUR...

THE BIG GALLEY, YEAH...

FOR THIS OPERATION YOU WILL EMPLOY THE CORSICAN PRISONERS NOW BUILDING THE ROMAN ROAD...

THE ROMAN ROAD, YEAH...

AS A REWARD FOR THEIR WORK, THE CORSICAN PRISONERS WILL BE SET FREE... BUT BE CAREFUL! I DON'T WANT THE GARRISON TO GET WIND OF THIS!

YOU DON'T?

NO, BECAUSE ONCE THE GALLEY IS LOADED UP WE'LL GO ABOARD OURSELVES, AND SAIL AWAY FROM CORSICA, LEAVING THE GARRISON BEHIND TO DEFEND THE EMPTY WAREHOUSES! HA, HA, HA!

HA, HA, HA!

YOU'LL HAVE TO WORK ALL NIGHT... NOW, IS THAT ALL QUITE CLEAR?

ER...

31A

NO.

NEVER MIND! DO JUST AS I SAY, AND YOU'LL COME BACK TO ROME WITH ME, BE RICH AND RESPECTED.

YEAH?

THE ROMAN ROAD BEING BUILT BETWEEN ALERIA AND MARIANA... THE ROADWORKS HAVE BEEN IN PROGRESS FOR THREE YEARS...

HEY... I'VE GOT WORK FOR YOU.

NOT JUST A TRAITOR, FOUL-MOUTHED TOO!

31B

36

THAT NIGHT, ON BOARD A GALLEY IN THE PORT OF ALERIA...

...AND ONCE THE SHIP IS LOADED UP, YOU WILL SAIL HER TO ROME. I SHALL BE ON BOARD WITH SALAMIX, WE'LL BE GETTING RID OF HIM DURING THE VOYAGE...

IT ALL HAS TO BE DONE TONIGHT... THE GARRISON MUSTN'T KNOW I'M ABANDONING THEM. THEY WILL FIGHT, AND THUS COVER MY ESCAPE...

AND AFTERWARDS YOU'LL GIVE US THE SHIP AND SET US FREE? THAT'S A PROMISE?

WHAT REASON CAN YOU HAVE TO DOUBT MY GOOD FAITH?

MEANWHILE...

RIGHT, GET WORKING. YOU MUST CARRY ALL THIS ON BOARD THE GALLEY.

TWENTY MINUTES LATER...

WHERE DO I PUT THIS?

AT THIS RATE IT'S GOING TO TAKE YEARS! AND WE HAVE TO STOP WORK AT DAYBREAK BECAUSE OF THE GARRISON!

THERE'S NO HURRY, BOYS. WE'VE GOT YEARS TO FINISH THE JOB, AND WE DON'T NEED TO DO ANYTHING DURING THE DAY.

I'VE GOT A COUSIN WHO HAS A JOB LIKE THAT, IN THE CIVIL SERVICE IN MASSILIA.

38

40

RAISE THE ALARM! RAISE THE ALARM! CORSICANS! MASSES OF CORSICANS OUTSIDE THE TOWN!

WELL, WELL! AND I THOUGHT THE CORSICANS WEREN'T GOING TO ATTACK?

WE'LL DISCUSS ALL THAT LATER! WE MUST MAKE A SORTIE OR THEY'LL FORCE THEIR WAY IN!

RIGHT, BUT YOU'RE COMING WITH US!

WE WANT TO BE SURE YOU'LL STAY TILL THE END OF THE BATTLE.

THIS IS MUTINY! YOU CAN'T FORCE YOUR LEADER TO LEAD THE WAY!

AH! ABOUT TIME TOO.

THESE THINGS NEVER START PUNCTUALLY.

I REMEMBER THE DAYS WHEN IT WAS A CONTINUOUS PERFORMANCE.

I DIDN'T KNOW THE PRAETOR WAS IN THE ACT TOO.

WHO... WHO ARE THOSE TWO?

I DON'T KNOW, BUT I'M NOT TOO KEEN ON BEING IN THE FRONT LINE!

CLAPCLAPCLAPCLAP CLAPCLAPCLAP!

I BROUGHT THEM TO SHOW THEM WHAT WE CAN DO, AND NOW THEY'RE GIVING US A LESSON! AND THEY'RE FROM THE CONTINENT TOO!

LET'S GO! WE CAN SORT IT ALL OUT LATER!

37

WHY DID YOU ACCUSE ME OF BETRAYING YOU TO THE ROMANS?

YOU WERE THE ONLY PERSON WHO KNEW I HAD COME TO YOUR VILLAGE... AND THEN THE ROMANS CAME ALONG DURING MY SIESTA.

FLICK! FLICK!

WE DIDN'T KNOW THEY WERE COMING. WE JUST TOOK ADVANTAGE OF YOUR SIESTA TO GO AND TAKE PROVISIONS TO COUSIN RIGATONIX WHO'S BEEN HIDING IN THE MAQUIS FOR THIRTY YEARS OVER THAT BUSINESS OF LASAGNIX'S GREAT-AUNT.

I REMEMBER! THE PRAETOR DIDN'T GET A TIP-OFF FROM OLABELLA-MARGARITIX. HE SIMPLY HAD YOU FOLLOWED, AND WHEN OLABELLA-MARGARITIX AND HIS MEN WENT OFF, HE TOOK HIS CHANCE TO CAPTURE YOU.

MAYBE... BUT THAT DOESN'T SETTLE THE BUSINESS OF YOUR GREAT-GRANDFATHER WHO WOULDN'T PAY FOR THE DONKEY WHICH...

STOP IT!

THAT'S QUITE ENOUGH PAST HISTORY!

YOU'VE BEEN FIGHTING TOGETHER AGAINST YOUR OPPRESSOR, AND YOU'LL HAVE TO FIGHT AGAIN IF YOU'RE TO REMAIN FREE, SO SHAKE HANDS!

CREAK! CREAK!

HURRAH FOR BONEYWASAWARRIORWAYAYIX! HURRAH FOR OLABELLAMARGARITIX! HURRAH FOR ASTERIX! LET'S HAVE A PARTY! OINK!

42

BEATING THE ROMANS IS NOTHING, BUT SETTLING A VENDETTA BETWEEN TWO CLANS IS AN AMAZING FEAT!

SUCH POINTLESS FEUDS WILL NEVER EXIST IN CORSICA AGAIN!

GOOD... AND NOW WE MUST BE GETTING HOME TO GAUL, BONEYWASÁ-WARRIORWAYAYIX.

WHAT WOULD YOU LIKE AS A PRESENT FROM CORSICA?

THAT DEAR LITTLE DOG.

HEY, OLABELLA-MARGARITIX!

?

WE AND COUSIN LASAGNIX WOULD LIKE TO KNOW WHERE YOUR COUSIN RIGATONIX IS. WE WANT A WORD WITH HIM.

I'M NOT SAYING, SPAGHETTIX.

YOU'LL BE SORRY FOR THIS, OLABELLA-MARGARITIX.

WE MAY NOTE IN PASSING THAT, AS A RESULT OF THIS RATHER COMPLICATED MATTER, ONE OF THE DESCENDANTS OF THE OLABELLAMARGARITIX CLAN WAS FOUND LAST YEAR BY THE POLICE, HIDING IN THE MAQUIS BEHIND A MOTEL.

43

PRINTED IN BELGIUM BY
proost
INTERNATIONAL BOOK PRODUCTION